Digger and Daisy

Go to the City

By Judy Young

Illustrated by Dana Sullivan

Text Copyright © 2015 Judy Young
Illustration Copyright © 2015 Dana Sullivan

Sleeping Bear Press™

315 E. Eisenhower Parkway, Ste. 200
Ann Arbor, MI 48108
www.sleepingbearpress.com

Printed and bound in the United States.

10 9 8 7 6 5 4 3 2 1 (case)
10 9 8 7 6 5 4 3 2 1 (pbk)

Library of Congress Cataloging-in-Publication Data

Young, Judy, 1956-
Digger and Daisy go to the city / written by Judy Young ; illustrated by Dana Sullivan.
pages cm. —
(I am a reader) (Digger and Daisy ; book 4) Summary: When Daisy the dog and her brother Digger go to the big city, Daisy shops and insists Digger stay beside her or he will get lost, but she will not go into the store that interests him the most.
ISBN 978-1-58536-847-1 (hard cover) — ISBN 978-1-58536-848-8 (paper back)
[1. City and town life—Fiction. 2. Brothers and sisters—Fiction. 3. Dogs—Fiction.] I. Sullivan, Dana, illustrator. II. Title.
PZ7.Y8664Die 2015
[E]—dc23
2014027159

For Benjamin Patrick Guilfoy
—Judy

For Lesa, who's a big-city girl.
—Dana

Digger and Daisy go to the city.

There are tall buildings.

There are cars and trucks.

The sidewalk is very busy.

"Stay by me," says Daisy.

"You do not want to get lost."

2

Digger and Daisy walk by a store.

Hats are in the window.

"Let's go in," says Daisy.

"I want to look at hats."

"Do we have to?" says Digger.

"I do not want to look at hats."

"Stay by me," says Daisy.

"You do not want to get lost."

They go in. Daisy looks at hats.

Digger and Daisy walk to
another store.

Shoes are in the window.

"Let's go in," says Daisy.

"I want to look at shoes."

"Do we have to?" says Digger.

"I do not want to look at shoes."

"Stay by me," says Daisy.

"You do not want to get lost."

They go in. Daisy looks at shoes.

Dresses are in the next window.

"Let's go in," says Daisy.

"I want to look at dresses."

9

"Do we have to?" says Digger.
"I do not want to look at dresses."

"Stay by me," says Daisy.

"You do not want to get lost."

They go in. Daisy looks at dresses.

Toys are in the next window.

Digger slows down.

He sees toy cars.

"Can we go in?" says Digger.

"I want to look at toy cars."

"No," says Daisy.

"Stay by me or you will get lost."

Digger sees toy trucks.

He slows down more.

"Can we go in?" says Digger.

"I want to look at toy trucks."

"No," says Daisy.

"Stay by me or you will get lost."

Digger sees toy trains. He stops.

"Can we go in?" says Digger.

"I want to look at toy trains."

"No," says Daisy.

"Stay by me or you will get lost."

Digger looks at Daisy.

Daisy keeps walking.

She does not slow down.

She does not stop.

There are tall buildings.

There are cars and trucks.

And the sidewalk is very busy.

"I must stay by Daisy," says Digger.

"I do not want to get lost."

He runs down the busy sidewalk.

Daisy does not see Digger.

But Digger sees Daisy.

He sees Daisy slow down.

He sees Daisy stop.

He sees Daisy look in the window.

"Let's go in," Daisy says to Digger.

But Digger is not there!

"Oh no," says Daisy.

"Digger did not stay by me.

Now he is lost!"

Daisy looks
this way.
She sees the
busy sidewalk.
But no Digger.

Daisy looks that way.

She sees tall buildings.

But no Digger.

Then Daisy hears something.

Tap, tap, tap.

Something taps on the window.

Daisy looks in. She sees blocks.
She sees balls. She sees many toys.
And she sees Digger!

"Come on in," says Digger.

"We can look at all the toys.

But stay by me or you will
get lost!"

Look for other books in the Digger and Daisy series

Digger and Daisy Go to the Zoo

"In this early reader, a dog learns from his sister what he can and cannot do like other animals on a visit to the zoo. . . . It's a lovely little tribute to sibling camaraderie. . . . [T]his work is a welcoming invitation to read and a sweet encouragement to spend time with siblings."

—*Kirkus Reviews*